GOTCHA!

GOTCHA!

by **Jamie Gilson**

Illustrated by **Amy Wummer**

CLARION BOOKS 🖤 NEW YORK

Clarion Books
a Houghton Mifflin Company imprint
215 Park Avenue South, New York, NY 10003
Text copyright © 2006 by Jamie Gilson
Illustrations copyright © 2006 by Amy Wummer

The illustrations were executed in ink and watercolor.
The text was set in 15-point Eurika Roman.

The lines of verse on page 34 are from "October's Bright Blue Weather"
by Helen Hunt Jackson (1830–1885).

www.houghtonmifflinbooks.com

Printed in the U.S.A.

Library of Congress Cataloging-in-Publication Data

Gilson, Jamie.
Gotcha! / by Jamie Gilson ; illustrated by Amy Wummer.
p. cm.
Summary: While trying to learn about spiders in Mrs. Zookey's class,
Richard becomes the target of Patrick the Pest's pranks.
ISBN-13: 978-0-618-54356-4
ISBN-10: 0-618-54356-2
[1. Schools—Fiction. 2. Spiders—Fiction. 3. Behavior—Fiction.]
I. Wummer, Amy, ill. II. Title.
PZ7.G4385Go 2006
[Fic]—dc22
2005030678

KPT   10   9   8   7   6   5   4   3   2   1

To Beatrix Blythe Gilson, born to be a writer
—Grandma Jamie

To the stink bugs in my studio
—A.W.

CONTENTS

Along Came a Spider

"**F**our," said Mrs. Zookey. She crossed her arms and waited. Outside our room, lightning zigged across the sky.

"Five," said Mrs. Zookey.

Thunder rumbled.

I blinked, but I didn't make a peep. Nobody did. Only a minute before, all the kids at Tables Two and Three had been holding our noses and calling each other stink bugs.

That's why the whole class now had to sit with our lips zipped tight while Mrs. Zookey counted to ten.

"Six," she went on. The thunder rumbled louder.

Over at Table Three, Patrick the Pest was straightening his red bow tie. He wore it every day. Today he had it on with a brown-and-green camouflage shirt that hung way down below his knees. It looked really dumb.

Okay, at Table Two, we'd been saying "stink bug!" too, but Patrick's table had been saying it loudest. Just the week before, Mrs. Zookey had put Patrick at Table Three, with the quiet kids. Already he'd got them in trouble.

Patrick grinned at me, reached into the pocket of his huge shirt, and pulled something out. I looked over to see if Mrs. Zookey was watching, but as soon as I turned my head, a rubber band hit me smack on the ear.

I yelped, "Ouch!" I turned around, but Patrick was looking at the ceiling, like he hadn't done anything.

Mrs. Zookey heard my yelp. "Seven!" she counted. Then she caught me with her eyes. Mrs. Zookey has this way of staring at you that stops you from doing stuff you shouldn't do. Tess was sitting right next to Patrick at Table Three. She leaned forward like she was going to tell, but he shook his head at her. She rolled her eyes but leaned back.

Mrs. Zookey had stopped looking. She was writing on the chalkboard:

ONE MORE ARACHNID

We were doing arachnids. They're all the spiders in the spider family. It's my new favorite word. *A-rack-nid.* It feels good in your mouth when you say it out loud. But I didn't say it. That would have been talking.

I rubbed my ear where Patrick had zapped it. He made sure Mrs. Zookey wasn't looking, and then he held up a piece of yellow paper with a red crayon sign that said "GOTCHA!!!!!" I'd seen it before. He made it the day he moved to Table Three. I think it's his new favorite word.

Patrick is trouble. He's not scared to do stuff. When he does something that makes him look smart or makes you look silly, he flashes the sign. Mostly he flashes it at me. A lot of kids laugh. They don't want him to "Gotcha!" them.

I could get away with stuff, too, if I wanted to. Right now I wanted to. We'd all zipped our lips like Mrs. Zookey said. What if I just unzipped my lips, but no noise came out? What if?

I crossed my eyes at Patrick and I yawned. Huge.

Mrs. Zookey saw my yawn. She shook her head at me. "Now, Richard," she said. I zipped my lips up. She turned back to the chalkboard.

"GOTCHA!!!!!" Patrick flashed his sign at me again. He and Tess covered their laughs with their hands. Then he leaned his chair back just far enough so that it *almost* fell but didn't.

Mrs. Zookey has lots of red hair. When she gets mad at us, she shakes her head and her hair goes from side to side. And then she counts. She counts really, really slow. She likes to count. She's always counting stuff.

No thunder now. No lightning. No talk. The room was just totally quiet.

I looked up at the paper spiders hanging from the ceiling. There were twenty of them dangling from strings. We had each made a different kind. Mine was an orange-and-black garden spider.

Under ONE MORE ARACHNID, Mrs. Zookey was drawing a great big spotted spider. It had two parts. All spiders have two parts. That's how you know they're spiders and not just insects. Insects have *three* parts. Spiders are definitely *not* insects.

WOLF SPIDER, she wrote.

Patrick locked his thumbs together and wiggled his fingers at me like they were wolf spider legs.

"Eight," counted Mrs. Zookey.

Ben passed me a note. *Watch out. Patrick is out to get you!!*

Ben is my best friend since kindergarten. And I'm lucky he sits next to me at Table Two. He was right. But no way I was going to let Patrick make me look silly again. I just stared up at my hanging spider.

Only seven of its eight legs were left. If it was a real live spider, it could grow another one. But mine couldn't. That leg was probably stuck on the bottom of some kid's shoe.

Patrick was watching me. I could tell. He thought I was scared to do stuff like he did. And so I did something I shouldn't have done. I knew when I did it that I shouldn't, but I leaned my chair back, way back. Way farther back than he had, even. I took a deep breath, and I blew straight up to make the ceiling spiders shiver.

Kapow! My chair crashed to the floor. Me, too. I bonked my head. It broke everybody up. They were all laughing with their lips shut tight. Even Ben had to put his head on the table to keep from cracking up. I guess maybe I did look funny waving my arms on the way down.

This time, Mrs. Zookey wrote my name on the chalkboard. While she was writing, Patrick reached in his big shirt pocket, snuck out a green gummy worm, and sucked it into his mouth. A minute later he stuck out his tongue at Dawn Marie. Half a sticky green worm was sitting on it.

Dawn Marie sits across from me at Table Two. She's not afraid of anybody. She raised her hand to tell.

"Nine," Mrs. Zookey went on.

Patrick smiled like he hadn't unzipped his lips at all.

"Ten," said Mrs. Zookey, finally. "All right, my dears," she went on. "Now it's time to take three deep, *deep* breaths and think about how to behave. Think about *No Name Calling.* Think about what it's like to be called 'stink bug.'"

"One." She held her breath a long time. Then she let it go.

"Two.

"Three."

There. We could unzip our lips and talk again.

"Now, did you have a question, Dawn Marie?" she asked.

Dawn Marie pulled her arm down. Those three deep breaths had stopped her. I knew she wanted to tell, but telling *could* be Name Calling. She shook her head.

Then she leaned over and whispered, "Patrick started it." Ben, me, and Yolanda, the other kid at Table Two, all nodded.

"Patrick *always* starts it," I whispered back.

"But you're the one who got caught," Yolanda said, pointing at my name on the board.

"Better watch out," Ben said quietly. A few other kids had started making signs like Patrick's, but Ben and I don't play "Gotcha!" We just play.

"I don't like Patrick." Yolanda said. "He wears that dumb bow tie every day, he sticks out his tongue, and he hits. I don't like spiders, either," she said, looking up at our paper ones. "They've got too many eyes and way too many legs."

"People," Mrs. Zookey said, "it's time to turn in your Spider Facts. Be sure to write your name at the top of the page. Then have your table captain bring them up to my desk."

I already wrote my name, so I drew a spider web next to it. "My spider poisons flies and ties them up," I told the rest of Table Two. "Then, when it gets hungry, it sucks out their insides like you suck a smoothie through a straw. I put that in my Spider Facts. Isn't it gross!"

"That's nothing. Mine is the Spitting Spider," Dawn Marie said. "It catches gnats with its spit. And you know how the mommy Spitting Spider has babies? She carries the egg sac around in her jaws, and the spiderlings hatch right out of her mouth. That's my favorite fact." She smiled.

Yolanda looked like she was going to throw up.

"Mine is all fuzzy and hairy and big enough to eat mice," Ben told us. "How gross is that?" He wrote his name in huge letters and gave the page to Yolanda. She was our table captain.

Patrick was listening. "Well, mine's the Black Widow," he said. "It's got its own spider website that I went to on my computer. You can watch it crawl. It kills people dead. Your spiders can't top that." He smiled his mean smile. "Gotcha!"

Yolanda shrugged. She picked up the rest of Table Two's pages and went up to put them on Mrs. Zookey's desk. When she got back, she said, "Patrick just stepped on my toe. And you know what? At recess yesterday I heard him burp the whole alphabet from A to Z. It was disgusting."

"Really?" Dawn Marie asked. "I bet I could do that if I wanted to."

"All right, class," Mrs. Zookey said, clapping her hands over her head. Outside our room, the sky was turning black. Rain splashed the windows. "If the weather clears," she said, "we'll still go on our spider hunt at Green Lake after lunch. This morning, though, we're going to talk about those spiders you wrote about and the creatures they catch to eat. Predators and their prey."

Patrick waved his arm. Mrs. Zookey nodded at him. "There are snakes at Green Lake," he said. "I've seen them. Fat slimy snakes that can eat you up! They're predators. But they won't see *me*." He held out his big brown-and-green shirt, and he smiled. "I'm all camouflaged."

"Ha!" I said. I crossed my arms over my Spiderman T-shirt. I'd worn it special. Spider Facts: I've got two legs and ten toes. I eat pepperoni pizza.

Crack! Boom! Just like that, all the rain in the sky hit our windows. This wasn't just clouds and sprinkles. This was *huge*. Outside it got blacker. Then light filled our room like the flash from some giant's huge lightning camera. The thunder boomed out right away. It was like this giant had started beating on a big band drum.

"It's *HIM!* Hide! It's the THUNDER MONSTER!" Patrick yelled.

The lights went out. Kids screamed. Kids yelled.

In the spring when we were in first grade, a

tornado hit our town. The sky turned all green. It sucked the roof right off a kid's house. What if . . .

"Now, now," Mrs. Zookey said. "No need to be afraid. We're quite safe inside. Let's move away from the windows, though, to the story corner. One . . . Two . . . Three."

"If we're so safe," Ben asked me, "why does she want us to move?"

BIG HUGE thunder clap. *Ka-boom!* I jumped a foot and saw Patrick dive under Table Three. He must have been really scared. He curled up small. He hid his head under his arms like in tornado drills.

Even in the dark I could see him. I smiled. Guess what? It was my turn to go "Gotcha!" I dropped to my knees.

"Come on," Ben said, heading off to the story corner. I shook my head. Ben had said Patrick was out to get me, but what if I got him first? Then maybe he'd stop. If I did one last huge "Gotcha!," maybe he wouldn't say it anymore. Quiet as a snake, I started crawling toward Patrick. I could hear him breathe.

Then, right under the table, I found something I thought was gone forever. It was my spider's lost paper leg. When I picked it up, I knew exactly what I would do.

I crawled closer without making a sound. Patrick's shirt was big. The collar hung way back from his neck. Slowly, I reached out. Then light, like a leaf, I tickled his neck with the leg of my spider.

He jumped. He shivered. He yelped a little yelp. Then he curled up tighter. Outside I could hear the wind howl. Then quietly, quietly, I sang in his ear, "The humongous tongue-less spider crawled up the monster's snout."

Yes!

Predator or Prey?

Patrick uncurled. Fast. He turned and hit me *Pow!* in the nose with his elbow.

The lights came back on in Mrs. Zookey's room. Kids cheered. I leaned my back against a chair. My eyes were running. So was my nose.

Patrick crawled out of his table cave and said to me, "You thought I was scared. Ha!" The kids in the story corner were looking at us. I *knew* he was scared. I could tell. He was shaking.

He scooted over and sang in my ear, "The monster sneezed out snot and washed the spider out."

The lights went off again. Patrick put his hands over his face.

The lights came on again. Patrick slowly stood up and folded his arms. "You thought you could get me," he said. "Not."

He looked at the kids who were watching us. "You know what I just did under the table?" he asked them. "I squashed an eensy-weensy spider." He smiled. He didn't even need to say "Gotcha!"

I didn't tell on Patrick. Patrick didn't tell on me. But I knew and he knew. Ben knew, too, because he'd seen me crawl under the table.

"All clear," Mrs. Zookey called. "Everyone back to your table."

"Your nose is bleeding," Ben whispered. "You're a mess."

I ran to the sink with my head tilted back. I splashed my face clean and dried it off with paper towels. Then I stuck a tissue under my nose and looked in the mirror. Ben was right. I was a mess. My nose looked like I'd been hit by a line drive.

We could still hear the thunder, but now it wasn't a monster. Or if it was, it was far, far away.

Just as I sat down, our principal, Mr. Prothero,

poked his head into the room. He was huffing. Mr. Prothero is nice. He isn't scary. Mr. Prothero is round in the middle. Last Halloween he dressed up in a polka-dot suit like a fat, funny clown. He didn't need to add a pillow. "Everything all right in here?" he asked. He asked it loud. Mr. Prothero never needs a bullhorn.

"Yes, Mr. Prothero," we said, all together. Mr. Prothero likes it when we answer him all together.

He stepped inside. "And you, Richard?" he asked me. "You look as though you've been in a scrap."

"I'm okay," I told him. "I just bumped into something in the dark." The kids looked at my nose and then they looked at Patrick. Patrick was grinning. Another "Gotcha!" for Patrick.

"No more problems on that front," Mr. Prothero went on. "We're out of the dark for now. You can all see where you're going. The weather service tells us the storm is speeding away, but recess will be inside today."

Kids groaned. There'd be awesome puddles out there.

Then Mr. Prothero boomed out, "Sumac School Is Best in State!" We knew that one.

"Sumac School Is Really Great," we answered all together.

"I can't hear you!" he shouted.

"*Sumac School Is Really Great!*" we yelled.

"And Mr. P. is overweight!" Patrick whispered. Patrick tries to make everything funny. Tess and some other kids giggled.

I don't think Mr. Prothero heard. If he did, he didn't care. He smiled and waved us goodbye.

"Well," Mrs. Zookey said, "we'll just have to make do inside. But that's okay. I've got a game I've been wanting to play with you. It's called Predator and Prey. Who can remember what a predator is?"

"It's somebody who catches somebody else," Patrick called out, pointing to himself. Most of the kids laughed.

Ben waved his hand. "No, it's one animal that eats another animal," he said.

"It's both," Mrs. Zookey told us. "Animals that catch and eat other animals are predators. And the prey?"

"They're the ones that get caught," I said. I rubbed my nose. The kids at Table Three giggled. Patrick didn't even need to flash his "GOTCHA!!!!!" at me.

"I, personally, think predators are mean," Yolanda told Mrs. Zookey.

"A predator has to catch food if it's going to eat, and it has to eat to live," Mrs. Zookey explained. "Is that mean?"

Yolanda frowned. "Maybe not. Not if it doesn't mean to be mean."

"In this game," Mrs. Zookey told us, "each of you will be a spider catching flies."

"Me, a spider? This is not good," Yolanda said.

"After we catch them, do we get to eat them?" I asked. I licked my lips. "Yum."

Yolanda rolled her eyes at me.

Mrs. Zookey smiled. "If you like," she answered.

"Yuck!" we all went, but for once Mrs. Zookey didn't go, "Shush." She just smiled again.

"I'll be a vegetarian spider," Yolanda whispered.

"No such thing," I told her. "They all eat meat."

"Do I get to spin a trap?" Ben asked.

"Not all spiders catch their prey in webs," Mrs. Zookey told him. "The ones you're going to be don't use webs."

Sam at Table One waved his hand. "Sometimes they jump on bugs. My Zebra Spider does. It's one of my Spider Facts. He can jump forty times longer than he is. I can't even jump two times longer than I am. I tried."

"I bet I . . . " Patrick started, but when we all turned to look at him, he stopped. He shrugged his shoulders. "Nobody could. Except maybe if you lived on the moon," he said.

"You are spiders that will sit still," Mrs. Zookey said. "No jumping at all." She reached up on a high shelf behind her desk and lifted something down. "A spider spends its whole life trying to catch enough food to stay alive," she told us. "What do you call a creature who does that?"

Patrick stood up and yelled, "Hungry!"

"Calm down, Patrick," Mrs. Zookey said, but she laughed anyway. She didn't even write his name on the board.

"Class?"

"Predator," we said all together.

"Right. A spider is programmed to be a predator. It can't help going after its prey. It's born knowing how."

She showed us the something she'd lifted

down. It was a folded-up bed sheet all printed with purple flowers. She flapped it open and spread it in the story corner like she was going to, maybe, take a nap there.

"Come sit in a circle around the edges of the sheet," she told us. Two kids were absent, so there were eighteen of us. We sat close together, our legs curled like pretzels.

Then she put something on top of the sheet. This new something was covered with a green towel. We couldn't see what it was.

"So, spiders, your food will come from here," she explained to us, patting the towel. "The rule of the game is that you have to stay put. Don't unwind your legs. I have some paper cups and paper plates. You can catch your flying food with these or with whatever you like."

Kids grabbed. I picked a paper cup. I looked inside. It was just a plain old cup. There wasn't anything spidery about it.

"I don't want to play this game," Yolanda said.

Ben put his plate on top of his head like a cap. Dawn Marie twirled her cup around on her finger.

Yolanda threw her plate across the circle. Tess caught it and sailed it back like a Frisbee.

Patrick said he'd just use his hands. Mrs. Zookey said that was okay with her.

"You have to catch your prey in the air, though," she said. "After it lands, it's out of bounds. No fair scooping any up from the sheet."

"Catch what?" kids were yelling. "Scooping what?"

"Flies?" Ben asked. "Really? Flies?"

"Flying food," Mrs. Zookey said. "But don't eat it right away. When we're through, each of you will count how many pieces of flying food you caught. Catch as many as you can. Ready?"

"Ready!" Dawn Marie and Patrick called loudest.

Mrs. Zookey pulled an electric cord out from under the towel and plugged it into the wall. Nothing happened.

We waited. We waited for her to say "Get set!" and "Go!"

We waited some more.

Soon we began to hear noises—*thump, thump, thump*—against the towel.

"Is this a magic trick?" I asked.

"Abracadabra!" said Mrs. Zookey, and she pulled the towel away.

Even before I saw it, I smelled it. It smelled like the movies. *Pop!* It was popcorn flying into the air. *Pop! Pop!* It was jumping up high, shooting out of the popper. *Pop! Pop! Pop!*

The popper didn't have its lid on. The popcorn was flying right and left and up and down. Kids were pushing each other, reaching out with their plates and cups.

Patrick bent toward the middle of the sheet. He tried to scoop up falling corn in his cupped hands. When he leaned back, he stuck his elbow in Ben's plate. All of Ben's popcorn flies fell on the floor. It wasn't a "Gotcha!," though, just an accident. "*Pa*-trick!" Ben yelled.

Tess tried to reach a wastebasket to use as a catcher. It was too far away.

I waved my cup from side to side. Sometimes I got a piece, sometimes not. I was getting hungry.

Dawn Marie opened her mouth and caught one on her tongue.

And then it stopped. The popping stopped.

"That's that," Mrs. Zookey said. "They're all popped up. Don't eat them yet. Now it's time to count how many you caught."

The middle of the purple-flowered sheet was

covered with popcorn. Some of it was scattered around the edges. I counted seven pieces in my cup.

"Zero," Ben moaned. "I got zilch! Patrick knocked all of mine on the floor." He grabbed two fat pieces from the sheet and ate them.

Yolanda lined hers up on the sheet. "Thirteen!" she told us, grinning. She was the one who didn't want to play.

"How many more flies did Yolanda's spider catch than yours did, Richard?" Mrs. Zookey asked. "Put yours down next to hers. You can see how many more thirteen is than seven."

One by one I counted them out on the sheet. Yolanda threw her arms in the air and called, "Six!"

"I caught one in my mouth," Dawn Marie told us. She stuck out her tongue and took the popcorn out to show us. "It's still hot. I spilled the rest. Do they count if you spilled them?"

"No," Patrick said. "You only got one. I grabbed one in each hand," he announced. "That means I got twice as many as Dawn Marie did. Ha!"

"Don't 'Ha!' me," Dawn Marie said. "Two's next to nothing."

Sam counted seventeen in his cup. That was ten more than I had, and way more than anybody else. Sam was a happy spider.

"Hooray for you all," Mrs. Zookey told us. "You got those flies. Spiders do that. And that's good. Real flies spread diseases to people. Spiders eat up insects that damage crops, too. Spiders are very useful creatures."

"Predators rule!" Patrick said, and he raised his fist in the air.

My nose hurt. I rubbed it. Patrick rubbed his nose to mimic me.

"Forget Patrick," Ben whispered, but it wasn't that easy. Patrick had been out to get me, and he'd got me. Over and over. I had to get him back. Somehow.

"Count your catch and compare it with two other people's numbers. Then scoop up a handful more for a snack," Mrs. Zookey told us.

"Flies. A handful of flies for a snack?" Yolanda wrinkled her nose. "I don't think so." She scooped hers up and dropped them in the wastepaper basket.

"Delicious," said Dawn Marie.

All at once the sun poked through the clouds. It got all the way to the popcorn pile in Mrs.

Zookey's room. "The rain has stopped," Mrs. Zookey said, going to the window. "But I expect there's a rainbow somewhere."

"Yahoo!" Patrick called. "We're off to Green Lake!"

Say "Cheese!"

"**H**ip, hip, hooray!" Mrs. Zookey said when we came back from lunch. "The rain has gone away. That means that soon we'll be heading off on our spider hunt. Mr. Prothero is coming with us. And Patrick has brought a surprise."

Ben and I looked at each other. This was not good. Patrick's surprises were rubber-band zaps and pokes in the nose.

Patrick held up a plastic bag. He swung it back and forth. "My father gave us this. It's from his store. We get to keep it." He smiled. "That means you have to write me thank-you letters."

He stuck his hand in the bag, and what he pulled out was a camera. "At home, my mom takes pictures of me with our super-expensive superduper digital camera. She's got seventeen photo albums just of *me*. But this camera's different." He held it high so everyone could see. "It's an instant one," he said. "You push a button and out comes a picture." He pushed his nose and then stuck out his tongue. "Like that."

I had to laugh. Patrick can be funny.

Mrs. Zookey laughed, too. "We will certainly be making your father a class thank-you card, Patrick," she told him.

"And he gave us film to go with it," Patrick went on. He shook the bag so we could hear that something was inside.

"The camera will make a fine addition to our trip," Mrs. Zookey said. "We'll take pictures and make a big poster for our wall."

She walked over to the chalkboard. "I've made a list of some photo possibilities." She picked up a piece of yellow chalk and wrote:

GREEN LAKE PICTURES

SPIDERS, she put down first.

"That's because we're going on a spider hunt," Dawn Marie whispered.

"This," Mrs. Zookey said, "is what I'm bringing to put our captured spiders in." She held up a big glass jar. It had a lid with tiny holes in it. "I have two of them," she told us.

"Eee-yew," went the kids at Table Four.
DIFFERENT KINDS OF SPIDER WEBS
"Spiders are sometimes small and often well camouflaged. They are hard to photograph," Mrs. Zookey said, "but we should see lots of webs. We'll try to bring one of them home with us."

"Bring a web home? You can't do that," Yolanda told Table Two. "You'd end up with a ball of sticky goo."

Mrs. Zookey heard her and smiled. "You'll see," she said. "You'll see. And," she went on, "here are some other things we might want photos of."

A PLANT YOU CAN NAME

"It better not be 'Leaves three, let me be,'"
Dawn Marie said. "That's poison ivy."

A BIRD YOU CAN NAME

A BUG YOU CAN NAME

A SQUIRREL

AN ANIMAL'S TRACK

A SNAKE, she added, smiling at Patrick.

"That's a pretty good start," she went on.
"Plus you can take pictures of other things you
find amazing. I'll hand the camera around
when we get there."

Then she lined us up at the door with bus
partners. I got Patrick.

"No fair," I told Mrs. Zookey. "I want Ben."

"It's time," Mrs. Zookey told me, "for you
and Patrick to learn to get along. Today you'll
be partners. I want you to stick together."

"Okay by me," Patrick said with a big smile.

Mrs. Zookey patted us both on the head like
we were good puppies.

"Have I ever got something to show you,"
Patrick said. "It's the best, but it's a secret. I've
been to Green Lake before. My father took me."

"Me, too," I told him. And that was true.
"Lots of times." That was sort of true. I'd been

maybe twice. "I caught a bluegill once." That was true. "It was as big as my h—." Hand is what size it was, but hand didn't sound big enough for Patrick. I thought about saying "house," but that would have been a whale, and those don't live in Green Lake. "It was as big as my *head*," I told him, finally.

"Well," he said, "once I caught a snark as long as my arm."

"A snark?"

"It's like a shark, only meaner," he told me. "But that's nothing. My father showed me something. I bet you never even knew it was there. He told me it'll make the best picture of the day. You'll see."

Mr. Prothero was already in the front seat of the bus. He called us each by name as we went past. Dawn Marie, who was Ben's partner for the day, told him and the bus driver a knock-knock joke.

"Knock, knock," Dawn Marie said.

"Who's there?" the bus driver asked.

"Spider."

"Spider who?" Ben asked.

"Spied'er with my little eye, stealing cherries from a pie," Dawn Marie said. She and Mr.

Prothero seemed to think that was the funniest joke they'd ever heard.

They were still laughing when Mrs. Zookey climbed on. She was last up the steps, carrying her big blue bag filled with spider-hunting stuff.

Patrick and I sat near the back. I got the window.

"So, second graders, off we go," Mr. Prothero boomed out in a voice as big as he was. "We'll see a damp but splendid show." Mr. Prothero likes to rhyme.

"Mr. P. said 'Off we go,'" Patrick whispered. "He's fat as Santa. Ho, ho, ho." Then he poked me in the ribs.

I poked him back.

The trip to Green Lake went on and on. Before long, lots of kids were kicking the backs of seats and seeing who could burp loudest.

Then, from the front of the bus we heard Mr. Prothero call out in his biggest outdoor voice. He didn't yell "Cut it out" or "That's just about enough of that." What he yelled was "We're going on a *spider* hunt!"

Everybody got quiet. We knew that one, only it was with bears.

We answered him all together. "We're going on a *spider* hunt!"

"I can't hear you," he told us.

We yelled back. *"We're going on a* spider *hunt!"*

"Walking along."

"Walking along."

"Oh, look."

"Oh, look."

"I see . . . grass," Mr. Prothero said.

"I *see grass*," we echoed him as loud as we could.

"Can't go over it."

"Can't go over it."

"Can't get around it."

"Can't get around it."

"Have to go through it," Mr. Prothero said, swishing his hands together over his head and then slapping his legs, like walking fast through tall grass.

"Have to go through it," we went, swishing and slapping, too.

With Mr. Prothero leading us, we waded in mud, climbed over mountains, and even went through a haunted house. By then the bus had stopped at Green Lake. We still hadn't found any spiders.

Patrick and I were last off the bus. Ben and Dawn Marie were with a group of kids listening to Mr. Prothero. He had both of his arms out, like he wanted to hug the whole place. He said:

"O suns and skies and clouds of June,
  And flowers of June together,
  Ye cannot rival for one hour
  October's bright blue weather.

"That's part of a poem I learned when I was in grade school," he told us. "And that's what this day seems like to me."

It was October, and the sky *was* bright blue. It didn't look like a thunder monster had ever lived up there. There weren't even little puffy white clouds. But there were puddles all over the path.

Ben and I marched through one of them. We splashed water all the way up to our knees. "We're going on a spider hunt," we sang.

"I don't see any spiders," Yolanda said, "and that's a good thing."

"Oh, but they're here," Mrs. Zookey told her. "We didn't need to come this far to find them, of course. I've heard that wherever you are, at school, at home, or outside, you're never more than four feet away from a spider."

"You're kidding!" Yolanda stuck her hands on top of her head and shut her eyes tight like she was as scared as Miss Muffet.

"Come on, I need your smile," Mrs. Zookey said. She led her over to a big bush with orange berries on it. Then she lined us all up in front of it. "Before we set off," she told us, "we'll have a class picture." She reached in her big blue bag and pulled out the camera Patrick had brought. "Stand up straight and say 'Cheese!'" she told us.

"Cheese!" we all went, even Mr. Prothero.

When the picture slid out, Mrs. Zookey looked at it twice, looked at it again, and then asked, "Well, what's this?"

"Oh," said Patrick, running up to her, laughing. "It's really funny. I knew you'd be surprised. This is the best film ever! It talks."

4

Mommy's Sweetums

"The film *talks?*" Mrs. Zookey asked him.

"The thing is," Patrick went, "my father couldn't sell it. He's got a big box of stuff nobody wants to buy. He says it's still good. No problem. But the pictures all say things."

Mrs. Zookey laughed and held it up for us to see. I got up close. It was a regular picture of all of us making crazy "Cheese" faces. Under the picture, though, it said, in fancy pink letters, "Mommy's Sweetums."

"It says 'Mommy's Sweetums,'" Patrick told everybody. "Isn't that weird? And it'll say something different under every picture. This roll's for taking pictures of babies. It was either that or one you're supposed to use at a wedding. That one says stuff like 'Happily Ever After' and 'Cute Couple.' My father thought this one would get more laughs," he went on. "You're all Mommy's Sweetums!"

"Can I call you Mommy's Sweetums, too?" Dawn Marie asked.

"Look out! There's a *spider!*" Patrick yelled, and he pointed behind us, pretending to see one. Everybody turned to look.

"Gotcha!" Patrick said.

He thought he'd fooled us all. But he hadn't. Because right behind us was a huge spider web. It stretched from the tree above to the bush with the orange berries below. It sparkled like it was covered with tiny Christmas tree lights. Rain was caught like flies all over the web. The sun was shining through every drop.

"Isn't it beautiful!" Mrs. Zookey said.

"But where's the spider?" some kid asked. We all looked. There were a few gnats stuck on the web between the raindrops, and one ladybug. No spider.

"Maybe it's hiding," Yolanda said, "waiting for its next meal to come along."

"Or maybe," said Dawn Marie, "a bird was

flying by. It saw the spider, thought it looked yummy, and ate it all up."

"Predators rule!" Patrick said. "I'm a predator, too. Patrick Predator. I'm the best at catching. Mrs. Zookey said you're born with it."

"She said *spiders* are, not boys," I told him.

"Same thing," he went. He hooked his thumbs together and wiggled his fingers like a spider.

Mrs. Zookey had already moved down the path with a bunch of kids. "I found one," she called. "This one can come back with us." She handed the camera to Sam and gave one of the spider jars to Dawn Marie, who took off the lid.

We all rushed up to watch. Mrs. Zookey pinched the thread of silk the spider was hanging from. She pulled it free and held the thread out to show us. The spider spun more silk, and the thread got longer. Mrs. Zookey pinched the silk thread closer to the spider, but it kept on spinning more.

"Look how fast it spins out that dragline," Mrs. Zookey said. "You think I can keep up with it?"

She kept pinching lower, and the spider kept spinning more thread. But Mrs. Zookey was faster. She was reeling the spider in.

Sam took a picture of it swinging in the air. Finally, Mrs. Zookey lifted the thread right over the jar and dropped the spider in. Dawn Marie twisted the lid on fast.

"When we get back," Mrs. Zookey told us, "we'll find some bugs to feed it."

"Here," said Sam, waving the photo. "You can't see the spider too clear, but it's really good of the jar." Under the picture it said in purple letters, "My Baby Face!"

That was pretty funny. Patrick's film was okay.

Somebody found another web with nobody at home. There weren't any raindrops on it, either, and so Mrs. Zookey said this was the one we'd take back with us.

"Can I carry it?" Ben asked, laughing. We could just imagine Ben walking along waving this sticky spider web in front of him.

"I don't see why not," Mrs. Zookey told him. Then she took two spray cans from her big blue bag. One said "Starch" on it. The other one was white paint. Mrs. Zookey looked hard at the web.

"I don't see a spider. Does anybody?" she asked.

Nobody did.

"We're going to take this web with us," she told us. "But that's all right. It'll only take the spider about an hour to spin a new one."

First she sprayed the web with starch, *whoosh*. "That's to make it stronger and even stickier," she said. Then she sprayed it with white paint, *whoosh, whoosh*.

From her bag she took out a piece of black construction paper. "One, two, three," she said, and she pressed the paper right up against the web. She caught it, too. The little white silk lines stuck right to it. They were round-and-round and crisscrossed on the black paper, just like when the spider made them. There was even one very white dead gnat.

"We'll pin this to the bulletin board right next to our picture poster. Won't it look fine!" said Mrs. Zookey.

She flapped the paper back and forth to make it dry. Then she asked Ben if he still wanted to carry it. He said no thank you. So she put it between two pieces of waxed paper and stuck it in her bag. We really *were* going to take a spider web home.

"Let's break into two groups now," she said. "You can either stay with Mr. Prothero or come with me. But remember to stick with your partners and not stray from the path. That's important. We don't want anyone getting lost or hurt."

A girl spotted a bright red cardinal about to land in a tree at the top of the hill. Mrs. Zookey handed her the camera, and they hurried up the path. Most of the kids ran after them.

Ben and Dawn Marie, Yolanda and Tess, and I stayed behind. So did Patrick because we were partners. Mr. Prothero followed us, whistling.

"Mrs. Zookey caught the spider," I told Patrick. "She's not a predator, but she reeled it in."

"Sure she is," he said. "She's bigger than it is, and she had a catching jar. But if you're a smart predator like me, nobody catches you. Ever."

"Not true," Dawn Marie told him. "If a hungry lion saw you right now, he'd eat you for a snack. You don't know everything."

"Hey, look," Patrick shouted, pointing down. "What a weird paw print. I'm going to get the camera from Mrs. Zookey. She said we'd share it. Be right back with it, Mr. Prothero." He waved to him. "Right back."

"That's just somebody's shoe heel," I called after him.

But Patrick was off, over the hill. I should have gone with him, but he said he'd be right back.

I stuck with the rest of the kids and Mr. Prothero. He spotted a Monarch butterfly, and we all stomped on a bunch of crunchy acorns under a tree that he told us was an oak. We found one web. It had a spider that ran away fast up a thread when we touched its web with a leaf.

Then we got to the top of the hill. From there we could see Green Lake. Ducks were landing on it. On the other side was the fishing dock where I had caught the bluegill the size of my hand.

Down the path, Mrs. Zookey and the rest of the class were gathered around a low bush. Patrick came running back from them. He was swinging the camera in front of him.

"They already got five more pictures," he told us. "One of them is this cool web that looks like a funnel with a spider at the bottom."

"What's it say under the picture?" Ben asked him.

"'Bye, Baby Bunting,'" he told us. "Those kids say its daddy's gone *fly* hunting."

"Everybody," Yolanda called. "Mr. Prothero found some fox prints in the mud. Over here, hurry!" Mr. Prothero was bending down, following the tracks over the top of the hill.

I started off to see, but Patrick grabbed my sleeve. "Come with me, partner. I'll show you something *really* good. Remember I told you about that secret place by the water?" He started down the hill toward the lake. "Come on."

"Mrs. Zookey said not to," I told him. "She said stay on the path."

"This is kind of a path," Patrick said. "Besides, she won't care. It's nature. It's a vine. It's a *grapevine*. I brought the camera back so you could take my picture riding on it. My father *said* to, and he's the one who gave us the camera. Come on."

"Is this a 'Gotcha!'?" I asked him. "Are you trying to get me? Because if you are . . ."

"You're just chicken. What are you so scared of? All you've got to do is point the camera and shoot." And he headed down the hill through the bushes.

The rest of our group was over the hill looking for fox tracks with Mr. Prothero. And Mrs.

Zookey had said I *had* to stick with Patrick. I followed him down the kind of path. He couldn't call me chicken.

Patrick was fast. Before I got halfway down the hill, he was already standing next to a big tree that leaned out over the lake. He'd put the camera on the ground and grabbed a long vine that was hanging from one of its branches. "This is it. This is what you swing on. I did it last summer about a hundred million times. Here," he said. "You first."

"Not me," I told him. "I'm just going to take your picture."

"Come on, you've got to try it," he said. "It's like you're a spider floating on a silk dragline." He pulled back the grapevine and swung it up to me. "*Cluck-cluck*," he went, and waggled his elbows like chicken wings.

I caught the vine. A lot of its leaves were gone. It had been used before.

"Now, hold on and swing," he said. "The higher up the hill you are, the farther you'll fly. You can even pump your legs. Go on! It's fun." He sat down on the bank to watch.

It did look like fun. Like on the playground, only better.

I shouldn't do it. I knew that. I should make Patrick go back up the hill. But if he could do it a hundred million times, I could do it once. He wasn't scared. I wouldn't be scared, either.

The sky was blue. The lake was blue. And I could do anything Patrick could do.

I backed up the hill as far as I could go. I held on tight, took a deep breath, started to run, tucked up my feet, and I flew. Like a spider.

Yellow leaves from the tree fell in the water as I swung out and back and then out and back again. The branch dipped down toward the lake, but I wasn't scared. I wasn't chicken. Not me.

When I landed, my heart was beating fast. I thought Patrick would say something like "Great job." Instead, he just handed me the camera. "Okay, okay, you did it. I didn't think you would. My turn. I'll swing out farther than you did. Now, make sure you can see me when you push the button. I bet Mrs. Zookey will put my picture right in the middle of our poster!"

Bossy Patrick. I almost started back up the hill. But Mrs. Zookey had said to take a picture of anything that was amazing, and I hadn't taken *any* pictures.

Patrick climbed up the bank as high as the grapevine would let him.

"Richard! Patrick!" I heard from the top of the hill. It was Mr. Prothero's booming voice. "What are you boys up to?"

Patrick let out a Tarzan cry and he swung out.

"Now!" he called. "Take it now!"

"Boys!" Mr. Prothero called.

I looked through the camera's eye. I could see Patrick pumping the vine high in the sky. I pushed the button. *Click.*

Then I looked again, without the camera. Patrick was holding on to the vine, but the vine wasn't holding on to the tree. It wasn't holding on to *anything*. It must have snapped when he was swinging out. No way he was going to swing back. He just kept on flying.

Splash! went Patrick. Just like that, Patrick went splash. He and his grapevine had landed, *plop*, in Green Lake, with all the bluegills and the snarks. I waited. I thought he'd bob up laughing, but he didn't. He didn't bob up at all!

I was scared. Really scared. I couldn't see him. I didn't know what to do. Patrick had sunk, and it was all my fault. I shouldn't have

let him come down the hill. I should have told. What if he never came up?

I ran to the edge of the lake.

"HELP!" I called as loud as I could. "HELP! MR. PROTHERO! HELP!"

Want to See?

Patrick could die. You can die in water. You see it on TV all the time. I couldn't see Patrick, but Mr. Prothero was puffing down the hill. He was tearing off his shirt as he ran.

I waded into the lake up to my ankles. The bottom was soft and ooshy. I was afraid to go deeper. It sucked at my shoes.

Now I could see Patrick again. I could see his head. He was banging the water with his arms. "Kick!" I called to him. "Dog-paddle!" Dog-paddle is all I can do.

Patrick didn't dog-paddle. He went under, but then he bobbed up again. I didn't know how to help him. I grabbed a long stick floating in the water, but no way it would reach that far. "MR. PROTHERO!" I called.

Mr. Prothero was already at the edge of the lake. He was pulling off his shoes and his pants. I couldn't believe it. Mr. Prothero was taking his pants off.

"Out," he said. "Out of the water, Richard. Get Mrs. Zookey. Hurry!"

I slogged out. My sneakers were oozing mud.

Mr. Prothero belly-flopped into the lake. All he was wearing was his underwear and green socks.

Patrick was moving away from the shore. He was hitting the water like he was mad at it. And he was yelling, "Get me out!" Mr. Prothero wasn't yelling, but you could see his bare arms windmilling fast through the water toward Patrick.

That's when Mrs. Zookey and the rest of the class came running back over the hill. Dawn Marie and Ben were in front. Before I was even halfway up the hill, Mrs. Zookey passed me, talking on her cell phone. "911?" I heard her say. Her voice was shaky. "We may have an emergency here."

Out in the water Mr. Prothero had grabbed

Patrick by his arm. The kids up on the trail were screaming. Then, when Mr. Prothero started towing Patrick toward us, they began to cheer. Patrick was kicking like crazy.

Soon Mr. Prothero had his feet on the bottom. He was walking through the water, his arm around Patrick, dragging him to shore. When Patrick started walking, too, everybody cheered again. Mrs. Zookey made her way down through the bushes to meet them.

I had to bite my lip to keep from crying. I was so glad Patrick was out of the water and not going to die. I didn't want to tease him ever again. I still had the camera in my hand. I couldn't help it. I took another picture. This one was of totally wet Patrick and Mr. Prothero in his underwear and dirty green socks. Underneath it said, "Smile, Baby, and the World Smiles with You." Nobody in the picture was smiling.

Then I looked at the one I'd taken first. It was pretty blurry, but you could still see Patrick and the grapevine flying through the air. Underneath it said, "Rock-a-Bye, Baby." It was true, too. Down came Patrick, cradle and all.

Next to the water's edge, Mr. Prothero sat on a

rock, putting his pants and shirt back on. Mrs. Zookey was climbing slowly up the hill through the bushes with Patrick behind her. She was back on her cell phone.

"No need to send an ambulance," I heard her say. "They're both fine. Soaking wet but fine." I ran ahead to tell Ben all about it.

When I looked back, Patrick was sitting in the grass. He had his head in his hands. I wondered if he was trying to think what he could say to make this funny. But when he got to the trail, he didn't laugh about a lake monster yanking him under or tell how "Mr. Proth-e-ro swam to-and-fro." He just ran to the bus in the parking lot. Water was running off his clothes.

Mrs. Zookey reached out, like she wanted to hold us all. "Oh, I'm so grateful," she said, "that nobody was hurt. You're all okay, aren't you?" She counted seventeen heads—twice. Then she dropped her cell phone back into her big blue bag.

Mr. Prothero passed us, pounding the side of his head to get the water out of his ear. His socks were muddy and he was carrying his shoes.

"Way to go, Mr. Prothero," Ben called, and Mr. Prothero stopped and waved.

"Life is an adventure," he said. "Learn to swim. Carry on."

Mrs. Zookey walked with him, talking, over to the bus.

We stayed where we were. I whispered to Ben about how I swung way out over the lake. "It was fun," I said. "Until Patrick fell, it was really fun."

"Of course, this means we're going back early," Mrs. Zookey told us when she came back. She shook her head. "That Patrick."

I waited, but she didn't say anything about me. I wondered if Patrick was going to tell that I'd swung, too. He could say it was my fault because I did it first.

Mrs. Zookey took a deep breath. I bet she counted to three. "I'm sorry all this happened, but our hunt was still a great success. We're taking back several pictures for our poster, one web, and two fine spiders." She reached in her bag and pulled out the two spider jars for us to see. They both looked empty to me.

"Can we give them names?" Sam asked.

"I don't think they'll come when you call,

but why not?" Mrs. Zookey said. She looked tired, like she'd really like to sit down.

"Can we feed them popcorn?" Yolanda asked.

"Not their idea of a snack," Mrs. Zookey told her. "A couple of nice fresh gnats or flies should do it. I'll show you how to catch them."

After Yolanda said "Yuck," Mrs. Zookey told us it was time to board the bus. The kids of Table Two were last in line. I handed the camera and my two pictures to Mrs. Zookey and climbed on.

Patrick was sitting in a front seat with Mr. Prothero. As I got on, he was saying something to Mr. Prothero. It sounded a lot like "I promise." I found an empty seat in the back.

When I looked up, Patrick had left Mr. Prothero and was heading down the aisle. His feet squished as he walked. He stopped beside me. "Can I have the window?" he asked. I guessed I was still his bus partner. I stood up and let him go by. A twig with little purple grapes the size of peas was stuck in his red bow tie. He sat down and his pants oozed lake water. I scooted to the very edge of the seat.

"Okay," he said, finally. "You got away with it and I didn't. Aren't you going to say 'Gotcha!'?"

I shook my head. "That's a mean game," I told him.

Ever since he had started "Gotcha!," I wanted to get Patrick like he got me. I *tried*. But when Patrick went under the water, I got scared. I got so scared, I stopped wanting to get him. I bet he felt like that, too. "It's a silly game. I'm not playing anymore," I told him. "No more 'Gotcha!' Right?"

Patrick laughed. "Okay by me," he said. The puddle on our seat was growing. I moved over farther. "I've got another game," he told me. "You want to play?" And then he called out, "We went on a spider hunt!" He said it loud. Kids turned around, but nobody said anything back.

"We went on a spider hunt!" Patrick said again, so loud I covered my ears.

"So we did," Mr. Prothero boomed from the front. "We went on a spider hunt." The kids in the bus echoed him.

"Walking along," Patrick shouted.

"Walking along," we all said.

"I can't hear you," Patrick shouted. "Walking along."

"*Walking along!*" we shouted back.

"Up a hill."

"Up a hill."

"I see a spider." Patrick got up on his knees. A lot of kids turned to look at him. He pointed.

"I see a spider." We pointed, too.

"Catch it if you can." And he pinched the air like Mrs. Zookey had pinched the spider's thread to catch it.

"Catch it if you can." We pinched the air, too.

"Walking along."

"Walking along."

"Oh, look."

"Oh, look."

"I see . . . water," Patrick said. Kids started to laugh.

"I see water," we shouted.

"Can't go over it."

"Can't go over it."

"Can't get around it."

"Can't get around it."

"Have to go through it." Patrick moved his arms like he was swimming. His floppy shirt was dripping. I moved to the way, way edge of the seat to keep from getting my pants wet.

"Have to go through it." The whole bus was swimming.

We waited for the next line.

Patrick stood up. You're not supposed to stand up while the bus is moving, but Patrick stood up. "I told Mr. Prothero I'd say I'm sorry to everybody, and I am. I'm sorry about what I did. I won't do that again."

"*And he won't do that again*," some kids said after him. I didn't say it. I wasn't so sure.

"Thank you, Patrick," Mrs. Zookey called, from her seat in the front. "Thank you for apologizing. And thank you all. We found excellent spiders on our spider hunt and butterflies and cardinals and—"

"—and one fish who couldn't swim," called Patrick. Kids laughed.

Patrick had said he was sorry. And he'd thought of a way to make it funny.

I thought it was funny that Mr. Prothero swam in his underwear. "What I want to know," I asked Patrick, "is why Mr. Prothero took his pants off."

"So he wouldn't sink—that's why," Patrick told me. "Wet clothes are really heavy. Shoes, too. He explained it to me. And if he'd sunk, we'd both have gone under. I guess he's pretty smart."

"Pretty brave, too," I told him.

We were almost back to school, and I was almost all the way off the wet seat when I said, "I was scared."

I thought Patrick might poke his elbow in my ribs, so I'd *have* to poke back, but he didn't. He waited.

"I was scared, too," he said. "So was Mr. Prothero. He told me. He's not mad, exactly, but he's going to call my father to come get me to see if I got hurt. Which, of course, I didn't."

"Then he's not going to throw you out of school or anything?" I asked him.

He shook his head. "You know what?" Patrick said, looking serious. "Sumac School *is* best in state, and Mr. P. is *really* great." It sounded like he meant it, too. Mr. Prothero had saved him, and he knew it.

I decided that going under in the deep, deep lake had changed Patrick. He wasn't going to be Patrick the Pest anymore.

Then, just as the bus drove up in front of the school, he said, "Oh, I forgot. I found something on the way up the hill from the lake. Want to see?" He unbuttoned the big top pocket of his soggy shirt. He opened it wide, and I leaned over to look.

Something poked out.

It was a head. The head was part of a squirmy brown snake. It stuck out its tongue at me. I jumped. I fell off the edge of my seat. I fell splat on the wet bus floor.

Patrick buttoned the pocket back up. "Gotcha!" he said.

No Way

I took a deep breath and counted to three.

"Patrick," I said. "You are *too* much trouble. I mean it. You said no more 'Gotcha!'"

"Did not," he said. "*You* said no more 'Gotcha!' I just said that was okay by me. I didn't say *no more* by me. Ha!"

We walked together, Patrick and me. My pants and feet were wet, but he was soaked all over. Splashing down in the deep, deep lake didn't scare the mean out of him. He was still Patrick the Pest.

When we got back to the room, I didn't tell about the snake in Patrick's pocket. I didn't even tell Ben, and I tell him *everything*. It would have been too "Gotcha!" I had promised.

I sat in my wet seat with my muddy shoes at Table Two with my arms crossed. Patrick had to wait for his father to come and pick him up.

"I'll tack some of the pictures we took up on the bulletin board," Mrs. Zookey said. "That way we can show Patrick's dad what we did with the camera he so kindly gave us."

She put up the picture of the whole class and pictures of spider webs, fox tracks, and a very red cardinal. She even pinned up the picture of Patrick sailing out over the water. All of them had silly sayings under them. She left off the one of Mr. Prothero in his socks and underwear.

"And here's one you and Richard didn't see, Patrick," Mrs. Zookey said, pinning it at the bottom. "Why don't you tell them about it, Sam."

"Mrs. Zookey found them," Sam said. "They were under a log. It was the grossest thing I ever saw."

"Was *not*," Tess said. "It was amazing. They were really camouflaged."

I looked up at the bulletin board. I couldn't tell what "they" were. A bunch of worms, maybe.

I didn't want to stand up to look because my pants were wet.

Patrick was closer. "Snakes," he said. "You found snakes."

"Garter snakes," Sam told him. "A zillion of them."

"A den of them," Mrs. Zookey told us. "Eight, maybe ten altogether."

"I wanted to bring one back," Tess said. "Patrick would have loved it. I wanted to, but Mrs. Zookey said no."

Patrick smiled.

I didn't say anything. I knew what Patrick had in his shirt pocket. He had two things. He had a little curled-up snake, and he had a wet paper sign that said "GOTCHA!!!!!"

"We brought spiders back," Mrs. Zookey went on. "And a spider web. We've had gerbils in our class. Once we had a rabbit to watch. But I said we couldn't bring one of the garter snakes with us. Why not?"

Kids' hands were waving. Lots of kids' hands were waving for Mrs. Zookey to call on them. Sam was almost throwing his arm at her. "Okay, Sam," she said. "Why not? Are they poisonous?"

"No," Patrick broke in, grinning. "I know that!"

"Not that, not that," Sam said. "You told us they *stink!* You said if you catch them and they get really scared, sometimes they let off this stinky, greasy oil. You said it's hard to get off, it stinks so much."

"Musk," Mrs. Zookey said. "The smell is called musk. The smell is so strong that if a fox catches a garter snake, it might even think it's dead and just drop it."

Patrick stopped smiling. He put his hand over his pocket.

Maybe the snake had been asleep, curled up in his big shirt pocket. Maybe his hand woke it up and it panicked. Maybe he pressed it on the "GOTCHA!!!!!" sign. Something sure happened, anyway. A disgusting, stinky smell was coming from Patrick's pocket.

Suddenly, all of us in Mrs. Zookey's class were holding our noses. Mrs. Zookey, too. Everybody looked at Patrick.

Patrick did not look back. He unbuttoned his pocket and pulled the snake out by its tail. It wiggled a lot. He held it up for us all to see. It was a brown snake with yellow stripes. It must have been plenty mad that it couldn't get free.

"You have a garter snake, Patrick," Mrs. Zookey said. "Don't let it loose." She picked up a pad of paper and started fanning the air. The spiders on the ceiling moved back and forth. Dawn Marie's Spitting Spider let go and floated to the floor. It landed right at Patrick's feet.

Mrs. Zookey didn't reach out to take the wiggly snake. Nobody did. We all stepped back. Nobody wanted to smell like Patrick. His bottom lip shook. He didn't cry, but he looked like he wanted to.

"But, but, what am I going to *do* with it?" Patrick asked. He was holding the snake away from him. It was trying to do a somersault.

"I know," Dawn Marie said. "I've got it. He could drop it in one of the spider jars. We could have an experiment. We could see whether the snake eats the spider or the spider eats the snake."

Yolanda groaned.

Mrs. Zookey took a deep breath. I could see her lips moving. She was counting. One. Two. Three.

"No, I think not." she said, finally. "I'll get a shoebox and punch little holes in it. It will be

the snake's box. You can put the snake inside, Patrick. Then you and your father will take it to Green Lake on your way home and let it go. Even if going there is a little out of your way. If the snake could talk, it would say 'Thank you' for doing that."

Maybe so, I was thinking. But if the snake could *listen*, I know what I would tell it. I would say, "Thank you, snake, for doing *that* to Patrick. Thank you big-time."

"You know what?" I asked Patrick.

He was just standing there, dripping, waiting for Mrs. Zookey to poke holes in a shoebox. "What?" he said.

"I think that garter snake already did say something," I told him. "I think it just went, 'Gotcha!'"

Jamie Gilson is the author of eighteen books, all of them contemporary stories that take place mainly in Illinois, where she has always lived. Her most recent Clarion books, *Bug in a Rug* and *It Goes Eeeeeeeeeeeee!*, are also about Richard and Mrs. Zookey's second-grade classroom.

A graduate of Northwestern University, Jamie has taught junior high; written, produced, and acted in educational radio programs at WBEZ; and written commercials for fine-arts radio station WFMT and film scripts for Encyclopaedia Britannica, Inc. For ten years, she was a columnist for *Chicago* magazine. Jamie is married to Jerome Gilson; they have three children and six astonishing grandchildren. She was born on the Fourth of July.